DISNEP · PIXAR
RATATOUILLE
(rat·a·too·ee)

Illustrated by the Disney Storybook Artists
Adapted by Caleb Burroughs

© 2008 Disney Enterprises, Inc. and Pixar. All Rights Reserved.

Published by Louis Weber, C.E.O., Publications International, Ltd.
7373 North Cicero Avenue, Lincolnwood, Illinois 60712
Ground Floor, 59 Gloucester Place, London W1U 8JJ

Customer Service: 1-800-594-8484 or customer_service@pilbooks.com

www.pilbooks.com

p i kids is a registered trademark of Publications International, Ltd.

Manufactured in China.

8 7 6 5 4 3 2 1

ISBN-13: 978-1-4127-9602-6
ISBN-10: 1-1427-9602-4

In a quaint cottage in the French countryside there lived a colony of rats. Remy the rat had the best nose in the entire colony. It was his job to smell the scraps that the other rats found, to tell if they were safe to eat. But Remy was tired of smelling garbage.

Remy liked good food. He did not like trash.

Remy wanted to be a chef in a kitchen. But his father said it was not safe.

Remy ignored his father's warning and crept into the kitchen that night. He hoped to find spices so that he could cook good food. There he spotted a cookbook called *Anyone Can Cook!* by the famous chef, Gusteau.

The old woman who lived in the house woke up. She chased the rats away. Remy got lost.

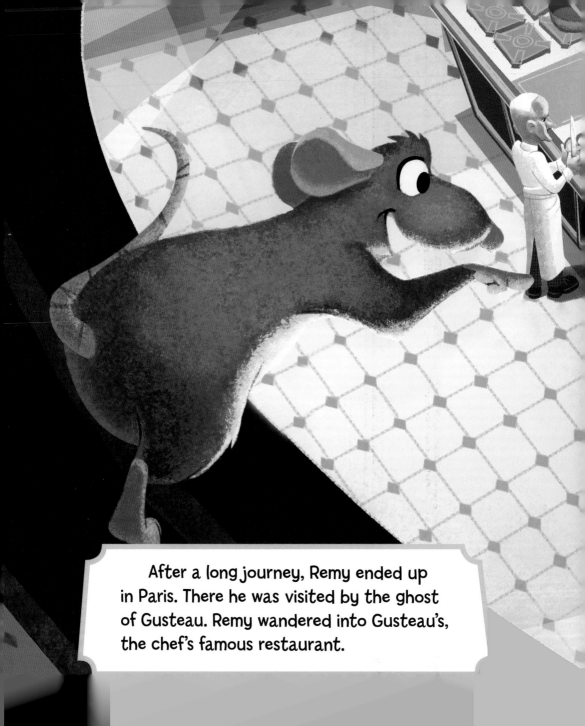

After a long journey, Remy ended up in Paris. There he was visited by the ghost of Gusteau. Remy wandered into Gusteau's, the chef's famous restaurant.

Remy hid. He watched the cooks make food. He wanted to cook, too.

While watching, Remy saw Linguini the garbage boy spill some soup. Linguini tried to make more soup, but it tasted awful. Gusteau told Remy to fix the soup. It was his big chance!

Linguini saw a rat cooking!
Remy's soup tasted great.
Linguini helped Remy hide.

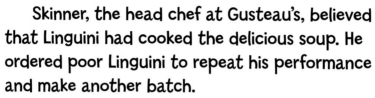

Skinner, the head chef at Gusteau's, believed that Linguini had cooked the delicious soup. He ordered poor Linguini to repeat his performance and make another batch.

Linguini brought Remy back to his apartment. They came up with a plan.

Remy sat on Linguini's head.
He showed Linguini how to cook.

With Remy's help, Linguini began to cook wonderful dishes. Skinner put Colette in charge of training Linguini to be a chef. At first, Colette did not like Linguini. But soon the two became close friends.

One morning, Colette found Linguini asleep on the kitchen floor. She was angry at Linguini and stomped outside. He was about to tell her his secret — that a rat helped him cook.

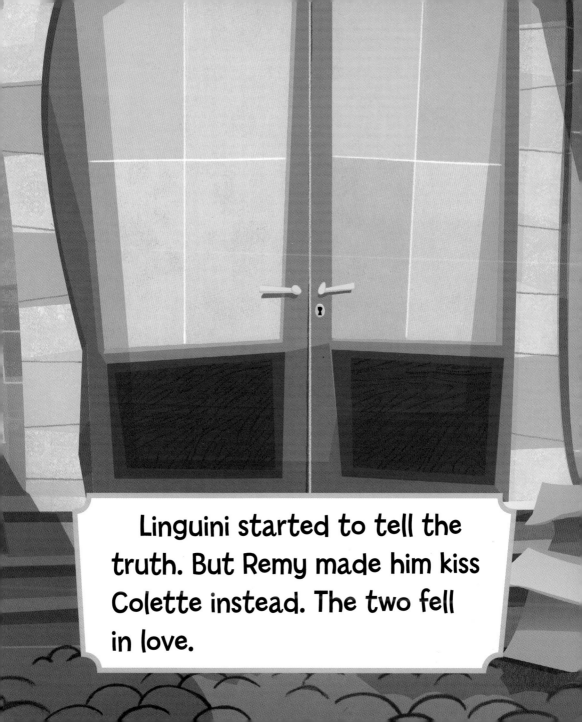

Linguini started to tell the truth. But Remy made him kiss Colette instead. The two fell in love.

One day Remy looked around Gusteau's restaurant. He found Gusteau's will hidden in Skinner's office. It said that Linguini was the rightful owner of Gusteau's!

Skinner caught Remy reading the will. He began to chase the rat through the city.

Skinner fell into the river.
Remy gave the will to Linguini.
The restaurant was now his!

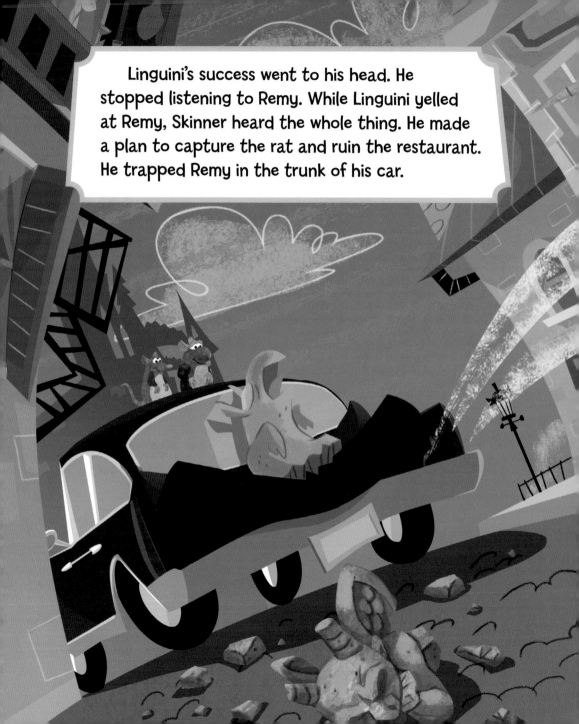

Linguini's success went to his head. He stopped listening to Remy. While Linguini yelled at Remy, Skinner heard the whole thing. He made a plan to capture the rat and ruin the restaurant. He trapped Remy in the trunk of his car.

Remy's family found him just in time. They helped him get away. He hurried to help his friend Linguini.

The rat colony helped Remy make a delicious dish. The meal impressed Ego, the grumpy food critic. With the help of Remy, his amazing new chef, Linguini opened his own restaurant, where the people and rats cooked happily ever after.